Ziggy
and the
Ice Ogre

Chris Powling

illustrated by
PETER FIRMIN

HEINEMANN · LONDON

William Heinemann Limited
Michelin House
81 Fulham Road
London, SW3 6RB

LONDON · MELBOURNE
AUCKLAND · JOHANNESBURG

First published 1988
Text © Chris Powling 1988
Illustrations © Peter Firmin 1988
ISBN 0 434 93051 2

Printed in Hong Kong
by Mandarin Offset

A school pack of BANANA BOOKS 25-30 is
available from Heinemann Educational Books
ISBN 0 435 00104 3

IF YOU WENT to Fountain City, you'd
see at once how it got its name.
Fountains. Fountains. Fountains . . .
everywhere. And not just ordinary
fountains, either. These were ice
fountains.

Yes, ice fountains.

The spray from each one glittered in
the air like frost turning a somersault
and when you stuck out a hand to catch
some, you soon had a helping of the best
ice-cream you've ever tasted. What's
more, it was always your favourite

flavour – vanilla, strawberry, chocolate,
hamburger . . . or maybe caramel,
chicken tandoori, steak-and-onion or
mint-choc-chip!

So where did this amazing ice-cream
come from? How was it made? Why
was it there at all?

Nobody really had a clue.

There was one guess, though, which
made people laugh out loud whenever it

was mentioned. Everyone in Fountain
City was quite, quite sure there was no
such creature as the Ice Ogre. 'The Ice
Ogre?' chortled the Mayor. 'My old
Granny told me about him. He lives
deep underground, right? And he's
enormous – so big that he could wreck
the city with a single hiccup. That's
what my old Granny used to say at any
rate. According to her, one puff of

breath from the Ice Ogre is enough to give a million people a slap-up, sit-down ice-cream supper. Imagine that!'

'Imagine that!' hooted the City Council. 'Our old Grannies told us the same story. Or was it our old Grandads?'

Either way, they didn't believe it. After all, who could possibly believe in an Ice Ogre?

So nobody bothered to look. Nobody ever found out that if you dug below Fountain City, beneath the parks and the pavements, the shops and the offices, you wouldn't have struck oil or coal or gold. Eventually you'd have struck Ogre. And since he was very ticklish, the chances are he'd have grinned in his sleep like a blizzard.

Nobody did I say?

This wasn't quite true. There was one

person in Fountain City who believed
every word she heard about the Ice
Ogre. Her name was Ziggy.

Ziggy was a street-kid. She lived in a
tiny ice-cream igloo (butterscotch
flavour) which she'd built for herself
right next door to a fountain – and
never once did she miss saying thank
you for being so lucky. 'Ice Ogre,' she

always declared, 'you're a good bloke!'
After this, she'd blow him an
ice-creamy kiss to show how grateful
she was.

Maybe that's why Ziggy spotted it
first on the terrible day when the
ice-cream stopped.

Plop! Plop! Plop!

Ziggy's eyes blinked open. 'What's
that?' she asked.

It was butterscotch dripping onto her
face and dribbling down her cheek,
straight into her mouth for breakfast.
'Thanks, Ice Ogre,' yawned Ziggy.
'You're a good bl . . .'

She broke off. 'Hang about,' she said.
Never before had ice-cream woken her
up – not at dawn, anyway. 'Hey!' she
yelped. 'The igloo's melting.'

So it was, slowly and stickily. But
when Ziggy hurried outside she saw

straightaway she had a bigger problem.
'Who's broken the fountain?' she asked
in dismay.

For there was no glitter in the air
now. The fountain was as still and silent
as a statue.

Nor was it the only one. As the sun

came up over the rooftops, Ziggy
discovered every fountain in the city
was the same. It was as if ice-cream had
never been invented. 'What can we do?'
Ziggy wailed.

'Do?' said a man on his way to work.
'Why do anything? I'm fed up with
ice-cream. Ice-cream all the time is
boring.'

To Ziggy's surprise other people
agreed with him. 'Blow the blinkin'
fountains,' they said. 'It gets on your
nerves scoffing ice-cream day in and day
out.'

By lunchtime there was even a slogan
chalked up on the City Hall. In big
letters it said,

WHO NEEDS ICE-CREAM ANYWAY?

That was just the trouble. About a
million people needed ice-cream. There
was nothing else for them to eat. Soon

they began to feel peckish. 'Know what I fancy?' someone said. 'A dollop of rum-and-raisin.'

'Or sherbert,' added her friend. 'I've always been partial to sherbert.'

'With me it's oxtail,' said someone else. 'There's something a bit different about oxtail ice-cream.'

All of a sudden they were hungry. Before long they were famished. Finally, a million people began to starve.

Ziggy was one of them. For the first time in her life she heard her tummy rumbling with emptiness. 'This is awful,' she groaned. 'What are you up to, Ice Ogre? This is Ziggy speaking.

Can't you see the trouble you're causing?' She said this crouching on her hands and knees with her mouth close up to one of the grids alongside each fountain. 'I know you're down there,' she called. 'Can you hear me?'

'Who are you talking to?' asked a passing policeman.

'The Ice Ogre, mister.'

'What, down a drain? Beats me how you can play games, kid, when the city's starving to death. Save your strength for staying alive, that's my advice. Everyone else is.'

'Everyone else has given-up, you mean,' muttered Ziggy. And as soon as the policeman was out of sight, she lifted the grid.

Ziggy stared at the tunnel underneath. 'Looks spooky to me,' she said. 'I'd better get going before I scare myself out of it. Here I come, Ice Ogre.'

Nervously, she crawled into the gap. At least, it started as a crawl. The floor was so steep it was hard for her to slow down. Soon she couldn't stop herself at all. 'Aaaaaaargh!' she yelled. In a cramped, cartwheeling, head-over-heels huddle that bumped her from top to toe, Ziggy fell deeper and deeper into darkness.

Shush!

She landed at last on something so soft, so crisp it might have been a drift of snow. 'It *is* a drift of snow,' she exclaimed. 'Wait, though. Couldn't it be . . . ice-cream? Yes, it is – lovely tutti-frutti!'

With a giggle of relief, Ziggy stuffed her face into a pile of it and slurp-slurp-slurped till her stomach almost burst. 'Ice Ogre,' she said when she'd finished.

'You're a good . . .' Her voice trailed away as she remembered where she was.

By now her eyes were used to the dark. Here and there in the gloom she could just pick out a shadow that was blacker and more solid than the rest. It was shaped exactly like a . . . like an Ogre? An Ogre so vast and knobbly he made you feel like a flea staring at a dinosaur?

That's how Ziggy felt. 'You're not just a good bloke, Ice Ogre,' she gulped. 'You're a big bloke, too.'

'The biggest there's ever been,' the Ice Ogre said.

His voice washed over Ziggy in a gigantic whisper as if he were afraid to deafen her or sweep her away. 'I've been

expecting you, Ziggy.'

'You know who I am?'

'You're the girl who always says thank you for my ice-cream.'

'That's me! So why have you stopped it, Ice Ogre?'

'Because it was the best way to bring you here *fast*, Ziggy. I need your help, urgently. You see, I've done something really stupid.'

'Go on.'

'I can't,' said the Ogre. 'I feel such a fool.'

'We all do daft things sometimes.'

'Not as daft as this. How could I be such a clown, such a goon, such an idiot of an Ogre? I was showing off, Ziggy, I admit it. I wanted to invent a completely new ice-cream, a totally fresh flavour. So I . . . I . . .' He broke off.

Ziggy peered up and up through the
dimness to where his head swung sadly
backwards and forwards like a mountain
being wagged. She half expected a tear
the size of a waterfall to come splashing
out of the darkness and swirl like a lake
all round her. Instead she heard a
colossal, gurgling faraway sniff. 'It was
pepper, Ziggy,' he went on.

'Pepper?'

'Pepper ice-cream, yes. The sharpest,
zingiest ice-cream ever invented. One
dab on your tongue and your mouth
explodes like a firework display. It was
my most brilliant invention – a stroke of
genius. I couldn't believe I'd been so
clever. Except I'd forgotten one thing.'

'What was that?'

'Pepper makes you sneeze.'

'So what?'

The Ice Ogre swallowed hard.

'Because some of it went up my nose, the way pepper does. Any day now I'm going to sneeze like a thunderstorm!'

'What and spread germs, you mean?'

'Germs?'

Ziggy felt the temperature drop all round her from the sudden chilliness in the Ice Ogre's voice. 'All Ice Ogres are germ-free,' he growled. 'Our ice-cream is so pure and so fine you never get fat from it however much you eat. Also you never ever get a single collywobble in your tum. Everyone knows that.'

'Sorry,' said Ziggy, hastily. 'What's the big problem, then?'

'Can't you guess?'

'Oh . . .' Ziggy said.

Suddenly she remembered the stories. If the Ice Ogre's hiccup was enough to wreck the city what would a full-scale sneeze do? 'I suppose it might cause a bit of damage,' she said.

'A bit of damage?' groaned the Ogre. 'Ziggy, I'll flatten the place! A sneeze from me is like a bomb, an earthquake and a flood all happening at once. When it's over there won't be any city left. This sneeze has got to be *stopped.*'

'How?' asked Ziggy in alarm.

'Don't you know? Ziggy, I was relying on you to tell me. If you can't . . .'

'Wait, Ice Ogre. Let me think . . .'

Being a street-kid helped, of course. Street-kids don't give up easily. Crouching deep underground next to the Ice Ogre's elbow, Ziggy wracked her brains for an answer.

How do you stop a sneeze?

How do you . . . ?

How do you . . . ?

How . . . ?

Slowly, she sat up. *The answer is you
don't. A sneeze can't be stopped
however hard you try.*

So you shift the city instead.

Ziggy took a deep breath. 'Ice Ogre,'
she called. 'Are you really the biggest
there's ever been?'

'I am.'

'Are you the strongest, too?'

'I must be, yes.'

'How nifty are you, then?'

'Nifty? What do you mean?'

'Well, do you think you could lift up all the city at once, Ice Ogre? So carefully that no one even notices?'

'*All of the city at once, Ziggy?*'

'That's right. Then put it down again just as carefully . . . except you won't be underneath it any more.'

'Where will I be?'

'Legging it to the North Pole as fast as

you can. Once you're up there you can sneeze as much as you like and it won't matter a bit. When you've finished you nip back under the city again and it's ice-cream on offer as usual. Of course, I realise it won't be easy.'

'Easy?' gasped the Ice Ogre. 'Ziggy it's impossible! Nobody is as nifty and strong as that.'

'You are,' said Ziggy. 'I'm sure you are. I've got faith in you, Ice Ogre. And I'll help you with the lifting – I'll guide you from the highest point in the city so you keep everything level. It's worth a try, isn't it? Besides, what else can we do?'

The Ice Ogre was silent.

Had he given up? Was he sulking? Could the sneeze have begun already? Ziggy held her breath and waited.

At last he spoke. 'Ziggy,' he said.

'You're right. It's the nuttiest notion I
ever heard of, but it's the one chance
we've got to save Fountain City. I'd
better puff you back to the surface
straightaway so we can get on with the
job. Quick, curl up in the tunnel like a
ball . . . are you ready?'

'Ready, Ice Ogre,' said Ziggy eagerly.

In a sudden gust of ice-cream, Ziggy found herself back where she'd started. It was as if she'd never been underground at all. 'Can you still hear me, Ice Ogre?' she called down the grid. 'I'll run all the way. Don't start until I get to Fountain Hill.'

'I'll wait for your signal, Ziggy,' came the whispered reply.

She didn't keep him long. Soon, panting for breath, she stood at the very top of Fountain Hill with the city spread round her like a giant map. 'There's nobody about,' she shouted. 'Not even that policeman. Good luck, Ice Ogre.'

'And to you, Ziggy.'

'On your mark then.'

'Yes.'

'Get set.'

'Yes.'

'Go!'

At once she could feel it under her feet and see it over her head – a whole city edging closer to the sky. 'Left claw down a bit,' Ziggy shouted.

'Like that?' asked the Ogre.

'Lovely. Now right claw up a bit . . .'

'Will this do?'

'Fine, Ogre.'

'Is my head in the proper place?'

'Spot on.'

'What about my shoulders?'

'Be careful with your shoulders, Ogre. I saw a whole row of houses shudder just then . . .'

'Is this better...?'

'Perfect!'

Slowly, smoothly, Fountain City rose in the air. From its deepest cellar to its loftiest steeple it was kept steady and safe by the best balancing act the world has ever seen – not to mention the best guide. 'Isn't that far enough, Ogre?' Ziggy called. 'We're at cloud level now, I can't see a thing.'

But already the mist was clearing as the city sank back into place so gently, Ziggy heard her own sigh of relief. 'Not a bump, or a scrape anywhere,' she exclaimed. 'Well done, Ogre! You've left it just the same. Nothing's changed at all except for . . . except for . . .' She gaped upwards.

Only the sky was different.

'Wow!' said Ziggy.

'Here what's going on?' came a voice. 'Oh, it's you again! what are you up to this time? Got tired of gawping down drains, have you?'

'See?' Ziggy pointed.

'Bless my soul!'

The policeman gaped, too. Who wouldn't at a sky full of Ogre? 'What is it?' he gasped. 'I've heard of a mackerel sky, but this is ridiculous! It's more like a whopping great whale!'

'It's the Ice Ogre,' said Ziggy.

'Eh?'

'He's turning north.'

'Do what? Leave off, kid. Not that Ice Ogre stuff again. Haven't we got enough to put up with? First the fountains stop, then we got this freak weather. If you ask me they're connected in some way.'

'They are,' Ziggy said.

33

'Good girl. You're talking sense at last.'

Ziggy shook her head but didn't bother to explain. What did it matter? And besides, was it over yet? The Ice Ogre should have been out of sight by now. Instead, high over the city, he seemed to be doubled-up.

Doubled-up?

'Oh no!' said Ziggy. 'Quick, mister – stick your fingers in your ears!'

'Sorry?'

'Like this,' she showed him. 'It's about to happen!'

'What is?'

'The sneeze!'

They were just in time.

A-A-A-A-A-A-A-A-A-A-A-TISHOO!!

The sky seemed to splash itself open.

'Look!' Ziggy breathed. 'It's . . .'

'Snow?' asked the policeman. 'Wait, that's not it. It's more like . . .'

'Ice-cream!' giggled Ziggy. 'What else could it be? We'd better get under cover fast!'

For three whole days and three whole nights, ice-cream fell on Fountain City.

As usual, it was germless, colly-wobble-
free and non-fattening. Also it thatched
every roof, clogged every gutter,
blocked every road and buried back-
yards and front-yards so deeply, every
house instantly became a bungalow.
Not that anybody minded. They were
too busy gorging themselves.

'Wonderful knickerbocker glory!'
some said. 'Kindly shovel me up some
more.'

'Make mine banana-split.'

'Neapolitan for me.'

'How about pistachio?'

'Brandysnap's my choice.'

'I prefer sharksfin.'

'Sharksfin?'

'Sharksfin ice-cream, yes. What's wrong with that?'

'Not a thing!'

But the real fun started when a million people felt healthy again. Icecreamball fights broke out all over the city with everyone eager to be hit.

Next came the grand Ice Ogre building competition. You were allowed

to use anything you liked for his claws and face provided you licked him into shape first. And if this got boring, there was always the ice-cream rink outside the City Hall with skaters trying their hardest to carve out figures you ate.

Best of all, though, was skiing down Fountain Hill. Here there were nursery slopes for the beginners, a slalom for the experts and even an ice-cream jump for the really plucky. The only losers were the ones who failed to crash. Never in a month of Sundaes had the city enjoyed itself more.

Or so the Mayor said. 'And I hope
they remember it at the next election,'
he told the city Council. 'After all, even
the fountains have started again now.
We're bound to get some of the credit.
Who else organised this Winter
Ice-Cream Festival – The Ice Ogre?'

'The Ice Ogre?' cackled the Council.
'What a laugh!'

Only one person in Fountain City
knew the true story, and she would
never tell it – not while there was

someone underground who wanted it to stay a secret.

Still, when Spring came round at last and most of the ice-cream had melted, she made sure she pressed her lips to the grid alongside her brand-new butterscotch igloo, and blew him an ice-creamy kiss. 'Thanks a lot, Ice Ogre,' she declared. 'I don't care a wafer what *they* think. I reckon you're a Good Bloke!'

'Bless you, Ziggy,' he whispered.

'Er, Ice Ogre?'

'Yes?'

'There is just one thing. I realise how you feel about fresh tastes and unusual flavours. That's great! And I really don't want to stop you experimenting. It's just that . . .'

'Just what, Ziggy?'

'Well, next time we may not be so lucky. So kindly miss out the *pepper* will you?'

'Atishoo!' said the Ice Ogre. But he was only joking.